Rookie reader®

W9-BJD-849

Messy Bessey and the Birthday Overnight

by Patricia and Fredrick McKissack

illustrated by Dana Regan

Children's Press®
A Division of Scholastic Inc.
New York Toronto London Auckland Sydney
Mexico City New Delhi Hong Kong
Danbury, Connecticut

**To Margaret Emily Haskins
—P. and F. M.**

**To Joe and Tommy
—D. R.**

Reading Consultant
Linda Cornwell
Learning Resource Consultant
Indiana Department of Education

Library of Congress Cataloging-in-Publication Data
McKissack, Pat.
    Messy Bessey and the birthday overnight / by Patricia and Fredrick McKissack;
illustrated by Dana Regan.
        p. cm. — (A rookie reader)
    Summary: Messy Bessey shows herself to be a true friend and a good guest
when she helps to clean up after a messy birthday sleepover.
    ISBN 0-516-20828-4 (lib. bdg.)   0-516-26411-7 (pbk.)
    [1. Helpfulness—Fiction. 2. Birthdays—Fiction. 3. Sleepovers—Fiction.
4. Cleanliness—Fiction. 5. Best friends—Fiction. 6. Stories in rhyme.]
I. McKissack, Fredrick. II. Regan, Dana, ill. III. Title. IV. Series.
PZ8.3.M224Md 1998
[E]813'.54—dc21
                      98-9223
                      CIP
                      AC

12 13 14 15 16 R 16 15 14 13
           62

Bessey was invited
to a birthday overnight.

She couldn't wait to get there
to share that special night.

Bessey joined the others who came to celebrate.

They had fun eating,

8

drinking,

dancing,

10

singing,

11

sharing secrets until late.

13

Then Bessey told a scary tale
to everyone's delight.

But when she ended
with a **SCREAM**,
it gave them all a fright.

When morning came,
the guests went home.
None of them seemed
to care . . .

. . . that pillows, puzzles, books, and games were scattered everywhere.

**But Messy Bess remembered
what every guest should know:**
*If you helped to make the mess,
clean up before you go.*

23

So Messy Bess got busy.
She found the mop and broom.

Then side by side,
the two good friends
cleaned up the messy room.

You're a good friend, Bessey.
It shows in all you do.

Nothing could be better than to be best friends with you.

About the Authors

Patricia and Fredrick McKissack are freelance writers, editors, and owners of All-Writing Services, a family business located in Chesterfield, Missouri. They are award-winning authors who have been honored with the Coretta Scott King Award, the Jane Addams Peace Award, the Newbery Honor, and the 1998 Regina Medal from the Catholic Library Association. Pat's book *Mirandy and Brother Wind,* illustrated by Jerry Pinkney, was a 1989 Caldecott Honor Book.

The McKissacks have written four other Rookie Readers about Messy Bessey. They have three grown children and live in St. Louis County, Missouri.

About the Illustrator

Dana Regan was born and raised in northern Wisconsin. She migrated south to Washington University in St. Louis, and eventually to Kansas City, Missouri, where she now lives with her husband, Dan, and her sons, Joe and Tommy.